for Joris

Hereafterthis

Adapted from a Folktale by Joseph Jacobs

Paul Galdone
drew the pictures

Library of Congress Cataloging in Publication Data

Jacobs, Joseph, 1854-1916.
  Hereafter This.

  SUMMARY: When Farmer Jan begins to ask his new wife what
she can do, a series of disasters follows.
  [1.2 Folklore] I. Galdone, Paul, Illus. II. Title.
PZ8.1.J153He4   398.2'2 [E]   72-12677
ISBN 0-07-022690-3
ISBN 0-07-022691-1 (lib. bdg.)

3456789 RABP 798765

McGRAW-HILL BOOK COMPANY
New York • St. Louis • San Francisco • Dusseldorf
London • Mexico • Panama • Sydney • Toronto

nce upon a time there was a farmer called
Jan, and he lived by himself in a
little farmhouse. By and by he thought that he
would like to have a wife to keep it all shiny and pretty.

So he went a-courting a fine maid, and he said to her,
"Will you marry me?"
"That I will, to be sure," said she.

So they went to church and were wed. After the wedding
was over, she got up on his horse behind him and he
brought her home. And they lived as happy as the day
was long.

One day, Jan said to his wife, "Wife, can you milk-y?"
"Oh, yes, Jan, I can milk-y.
Mother used to milk-y when I lived home."

So he went to market and bought her ten red cows.
All went well till one day when she had driven them
to the pond to drink, she thought they did not drink
fast enough. So she drove them right into the pond
to make them drink faster, and they were all drowned.

When Jan came home, she up and told him what she had done, and he said,

"Oh, well, there, never mind, my dear, better luck next time."

So they went on for a bit and then, one day, Jan said to his wife, "Wife, can you fatten pigs?"
"Oh, yes, Jan, I can fatten pigs.
Mother used to fatten pigs when I lived home."

So Jan went to market and bought her some pigs.
All went well till one day when she had put their
food into the trough, she thought they did not eat
fast enough, so she pushed their heads into the
trough to make them eat faster, and they were
all choked.

When Jan came home, she up and told him what she
had done, and he said,

"Oh, well, there, never mind, my dear, better luck next time."

So they went on for a bit, and then, one day,
Jan said to his wife, "Wife, can you bake-y?"
"Oh, yes, Jan, I can bake-y.
Mother used to bake-y when I lived home."

So he bought everything for his wife so that she
could bake bread.

All went well for a bit till
one day, she thought she would bake white bread
for a treat for Jan. So she carried her grain to
the top of a high hill and let the wind blow on
it, for she thought to herself that the wind would
blow out all the bran. But the wind blew away grain
and bran and all—so there was an end of it.

When Jan came home, she up and told him what she
had done, and he said,

"Oh, well, there, never mind, my dear, better luck next time."

So they went on for a bit, and then, one day,
Jan said to his wife, "Wife, can you brew-y?"
"Oh, yes, Jan, I can brew-y.
Mother used to brew-y when I lived home."

So he bought everything proper for his wife
to brew ale with. All went well for a bit
till one day when she had brewed her ale and
put it in the barrel, a big black dog came in and
looked up in her face.

She drove him out of the house, but he stayed
outside the door and looked up in her face.
She got so angry that she pulled out the plug
of the barrel, threw it at the dog, and said,
"What do you look at me for? I be Jan's wife."
Then the dog ran down the road, and she ran
after him to chase him right away.

When she came back again, she found that the ale had all run
out of the barrel, and so there was an end of it.

When Jan came home, she up and told him what she had done, and he said,
"Oh, well, there, never mind, my dear, better luck next time."

So they went on for a bit, and then, one day,
she thought to herself, "'Tis time to clean up
my house."
When she was taking down her big
bed, she found a bag of silver coins on the tester.

So when Jan came home, she up and said to him,
"Jan, what is that bag of coins on the
tester for?"
"That is for Hereafterthis, my dear."

Now, there was a robber outside the window, and
he heard what Jan said. Next day, he waited
till Jan had gone to market, and then he came
and knocked at the door.

"What do you please to want?" said the wife.
"I am Hereafterthis," said the robber. "I
have come for the bag of coins."

Now the robber was dressed like a fine gentleman,
and she thought to herself it was very kind of so
fine a man to come for the bag of coins. So
she ran upstairs and fetched the bag of silver
and gave it to the robber, and he went
away with it.

When Jan came home, she said to him, "Jan,
Hereafterthis has been for the bag of coins."
"What do you mean, wife?" said Jan.

So she up and told him, and he said, "Then I'm a
ruined man, for that money was to pay our rent with.
The only thing we can do is to roam the world over
till we find the bag of silver coins."

Then Jan took the house door off its hinges.
"That's all we shall have to lie on," he said.
So Jan put the door on his back, and they both
set out to look for Hereafterthis.

Many a long day they went, and in the night Jan
used to put the door on the branches of a tree
and they would sleep on it.

One night they came to a big hill, and there was
a high tree at the foot. So Jan put the door
up in it, and they got up in the tree and went
to sleep.

By and by Jan's wife heard a noise below, and she looked
to see what it was.

Along came two gentlemen with a long table, and behind them fine ladies and gentlemen, each carrying a bag. One of the gentlemen was Hereafterthis with the bag of silver coins.

They sat round the table and began to drink and talk and count up all the money in the bags. So then Jan's wife woke him up and asked what they should do.

"Now's our time," said Jan. And he pushed the door off the branches so that it fell right in the very middle of the table and frightened the robbers away.

Then Jan and his wife got down from the tree. They took their own bag of silver coins and as many moneybags as they could carry on the door and went straight home.

And Jan bought his wife more cows and more pigs,
and they lived happy everafter.